THE ROAD TO DAMASCUS

Richard D. Ramsey

Edited by: J. Ellington Ashton Press Staff
Cover Art by: **Michael Fisher**

http://jellingtonashton.com

Copyright.

Richard Ramsey

©2017, **Richard Ramsey**

ALL RIGHTS RESERVED. This book contains material protected under International and Federal Copyright Laws and Treaties. Any unauthorized reprint or use of this material is prohibited. No part of this book, including the cover and photos, may be reproduced or transmitted in any form or by any means, electronic or mechanical, including photocopying, recording, or by any information storage and retrieval system without express written permission from the author / publisher. All rights reserved.

Any resemblance to persons, places living or dead is purely coincidental.

This is a work of fiction.

1

My name is Jacob Mozel, but I've been called a great many things in my lifetime. Most of them, I'm not proud of; some of them I am.

"I am." Now that's a phrase that's haunted me most of my life. God refers to himself as "The Great I AM." Well, that's what he told Moses his name was. There was a philosopher once named Rene Descartes. He said "Cogito ergo sum." In English it means "I think, therefore I am." Does this mean that if we think, then we can become God; or is it more simple than that? I used to think that I knew what I was, only to realize that I was wrong. Most of my life has been about realizations and revelations. When I was a boy, I realized that the world, no, the universe, was a very ugly place. When I was in prison, I realized that I was not nearly as tough as I thought I was. And when I was asked to leave the seminary, I realized that man is fallible and can never be as divine and forgiving as God. That's all part of who I *was*, *what* I was; a pretty easy question to answer. So what am I now? I gave up trying to answer that question a long time ago. Who am I? I'm just an old person with a bible in one hand and a guitar in the other, waiting in this spaceport for God to show me the way.

***

I sat there for four days looking for something. I wasn't sure what it was, but I was sure I would know it when I saw it. Kids would pass by from time to time and ask me to play them a song. I've always been a sucker for an audience, so I'd pull an old folk tune out of my memory and play it for them. It's amazing that in this day and age a simple musical instrument can invoke awe and inspiration. We have technology that I'll never even begin to understand. We visit planets at the farthest reaches of the galaxy and mingle with aliens from other worlds, yet listening to a series of simple chords or watching water move still seems to hold a special place in our hearts. I know why, and that's why I'm here.

I rarely went hungry; in fact, I was sometimes rewarded handsomely for my songs and the occasional story. The food there something awful, but it kept your belly full.

When I was tired, there were bunks to be bought with just a little bit of coin. It was on the thirteenth day that I knew God was laying out his plan for me. It came in the form of a large ship called The Damascus.

As freighters go, it was smaller than most, older too. A single red line down the center of the hull was the only adornment. No symbols of the True Church, which was a good sign. Just the word Damascus, its Federal ID number, and a bar code monitor on the side. All cargo ships have been required to have their ID number written on the side under their names, but the monitor was a relatively new rule enacted sometime in the last ten or so years. The one on the ship dated it somewhat, it wasn't hard to see that the monitor here was an addition and not part of the original spec.

My heart raced as I watched the antiquated vessel come in at a sharp angle, alter to a rapid descent and land right at the docking port. Whoever piloted the ship was certainly a hot shot and not afraid to show it. It was not uncommon for young pilots to show off their skills when landing at the spaceports, it often caught the eyes of the young ladies and ensured the pilot would have a couple waiting to talk to him when he landed. This seemed like an amateur operation on the surface, but there was professionalism just underneath. Regardless of the pilot's age, I needed to talk to the captain; it was the only way I was getting on board a ship like that.

When I finally did catch up with him, he was not at all what I expected. Well, I don't know what I expected, but he certainly wasn't it. Maybe I anticipated somebody that was warm and friendly or someone that was personable since it seemed that that was where I needed to go, but Captain Stark was nothing like that. I had to ask around to find him. Many people in this port knew the ship, but they didn't know the crew. When I finally did locate him, he was having dinner in one of the local eateries in the spaceport, by himself.

There were quite a few things I found odd about him at first. One was that he was alone. Freighter captains rarely had a moment's peace in a spaceport that deep into the trade district. The next thing I noticed was that he was wearing jeans. Six centuries of human development and jeans just never went out of style, unless you were a wealthy businessman. His casual appearance was strange because I knew a man that ran any operation like that had to have a substantial cash flow. A pilot that skilled just didn't carry trinkets. He was tall and thin and had a bald head that seemed to reflect even the low lighting in the restaurant. He didn't want to be noticed, that much was obvious. In fact, there was nothing that stood out about him at all, except for one thing. He held his fork funny.

It wasn't something that was highly remarkable, just a subtle detail that seemed to bring definition to one's presentation. Most people from well-to-do homes or those who had a fancy upbringing would hold their forks like holding a pencil, or a drumstick if you knew about the old time drummers. Captain Stark held his in a closed fist. If I tried to eat like that, I imagine I would feel very clumsy getting the food to my mouth; but there was nothing clumsy about this man. He kept his eyes on his plate and shoveled the food in his mouth both gracefully and methodically. I guess you can tell a lot about a man by the way he eats. Anyway, I tucked my Bible into a secret compartment inside my guitar, experience had taught me to keep contraband such as that hidden, especially when approaching strangers. With caution, I invited myself into the eatery and approached his table.

"Are you Captain Stark?"

He put his meal on pause, looked up at me and said, "Yes I am" over a mouthful of food.

"May I sit down?"

He gestured to an empty seat at the table and resumed eating.

"You're the Captain of the Damascus?"

"Yes I am, but I'm afraid all of my bays are full. I can't take any more loads right now."

He got straight to the point. "I'm not trying to move freight, I'm looking for transport."

The Captain shook his head. "I move cargo, not people. You need a commuter ship. There are lots and lots of passenger ships that dock at the starboard concourse. You can find a transport there."

I smiled and rubbed my beard. It was amazing how fast it grew those days. It seemed to get longer and grayer all the time. "But, I really want to travel on your ship."

Stark stopped eating, put his fork down and looked me squarely in the face. "Who sent you here?"

I was confused; I wasn't sure what he was getting at. "Nobody sent me here. I just asked around to find out who captained your ship."

"Why would you have me believe that you want transport on a cargo vessel? Do you really think I'm that stupid?" His teeth were clenched and I could see his jaw muscles contracting in his cheeks.

I shifted in my seat. Convincing him was not going to be as easy as I thought. "I have no subversive plans. I only want to 'hitch a ride' as they said in the old days." I smiled real big and tried to turn on as much boyish charm as I had left in me at such an old age.

Captain Stark looked back down at his food and resumed stuffing it in his face. "Find a passenger shuttle. I'm a freighter captain."

As if to add an additional layer of finality to our conversation, we had an unexpected guest. She was an Inillian woman in a loose fitting leather jacket and skin tight cargo pants. I couldn't even guess as to how old she was, I didn't know my alien species that well. I had only seen a handful of them in my lifetime. A fascinating aspect of Inillians, you could always tell what was on their mind. They had a shiny fur coat with a texture almost as soft as a mink and the color of it changed with their emotion. This one was a deep black with layers of purple that rippled across her tender pelt like waves. She was not happy to say the least.

Her face was almost like that of a cat with less of a muzzle and no whiskers. Well, on second thought, not so much a cat; but that's the closest way I can describe it to you. She strolled up to the side of the table from behind me without a sound. I would have been startled if I hadn't been taken aback by her striking figure. I may be a priest, but I'm not dead.

Captain Stark set his fork down again and sat up straight wearing a curious face. He knew something was terribly wrong. "Jenna? What is it?"

Jenna. What a fitting name. When she spoke, her voice was as elegant as her fleece. "We're being boarded, sir."

"Port guards?"

"No, Transit Authority."

Stark wiped his mouth with a thick napkin and then threw it on the table. "Transit Authority? What do they want with us?"

That was the last thing I heard him say as they hustled out of the diner. I guess I was going to have to find a passenger shuttle after all.

The Transit Authority were a nasty bunch. They were responsible for monitoring shipments between space ports, looking for contraband and trade violations. Mostly trade violations between different governments. They were formed many years ago as an agreement between planets as a sort of police force to regulate trade agreements. It hasn't worked out as well as you would think. You see, they're an autonomous entity that doesn't answer to one government, but to all of them in theory. As you can imagine, this causes a great deal of problems for traders. I wish I could say that there was no corruption, but it runs very deep. I even had to hide my Bible inside my guitar to get it past them and onto the station.

The captain had left a large portion of his meal uneaten. I would like to say that I wasn't hungry, but I was. Tips for a song hadn't come through as much as they had earlier in the week. I helped myself to the rest of what could have been labeled as meatloaf but what would have been called something else.

Upon leaving the eatery, a busy scene was unfolding in the terminal. Captain Stark, Jenna and about eight others were lined up against a wall with their hands flat against it. Several Transit Authority servicemen were standing close by with some high powered rifles. It seemed a little much, but I'm no expert. One serviceman was making his way down the line, frisking each crewman. When he got to Jenna, he lingered a bit on her long legs. She pulled back, turned and hissed at him. Well, it wasn't a hiss as much as it was a growl with a tongue roll. Either way, her intention was clear and her fur was still a deep black. The serviceman rose quickly and brought his elbow up into the side of her face. She stumbled back and cast him a look that was laced with pure rage. A wave of purple rippled through her coat.

Captain Stark left his position on the wall, put one hand on her shoulder and whispered something in her ear. She nodded and they both resumed their previous stance.

A large crowd gathered to take in the spectacle. I stepped up to one of the sanitation workers and whispered to him, "What's going on here?" Sanitation workers seemed to be the best sources of information in those places. They went in and out of all situations without being seen or heard, but they were always listening for information that could be sold to the right person with enough currency. That one owed me a favor.

"The Damascus has been running prostitutes. Transit Authority's finally catching up with them."

"Prostitutes? Are you sure?"

"Sure as I'm standing here. Heard it was a bunch of little girls from Mo`ak."

I was very disappointed. "I was trying to get a lift on that ship. The name is… well, let's just say it has a special meaning to me."

"Ya don't want to get a ride on that ship. I've seen them come through here more than a few times. They're a hard bunch. Run a lot of contraband so I hear. You see how they have some of the crew on a separate wall?"

The crew was obviously being separated. A few were left with Captain Stark, but most were moved to the other side of the concourse. "What's that all about?"

"They're not registered with the Transit Authority. Every trader has to have a registration. Those guys are migrant workers, picked up at one dock and hired to help on to the other."

"What will happen to them?"

"Oh, they'll be detained for a couple of months and then they'll be released to do the same thing over and over. The authority likes it that way. It gives them a reason to do surprise inspections."

"And the Captain?"

"Ah, that's a different story. He'll be fined for hiring them and have some of his cargo confiscated. Now, if they find the Mo`ak prostitutes on his ship, he'll go to a penal colony for life."

With that, the entire crew of the Damascus was lead away in shackles.

I was out of money that night, so I found an empty bench in a less busy concourse of the port and tried to drift off to sleep. It was hard to rest, having seen that night's spectacle. A certain disappointed melancholy had settled onto me. I was sure that this was the sign that God had sent me. I guess I was wrong. I prayed long and hard, but it didn't help my fitful sleep or belay my unsettling dreams.

I was woken suddenly by a less than accommodating member of the Transit Authority. He shook me awake, cuffed me, told me I was under arrest and led me off. I told him I needed to take my guitar with me, but he didn't listen. More than anything, I was worried about losing my Bible.

They led me to a room where a man of some ranked importance was seated at a table. As a presumed measure of intimidation, I was seated directly across from him. He was an older gentleman, but not as old as myself. He had fat jowls that were really too well shaven and a large forehead that gave way to a pitch black flat top hairdo. His bottom lip protruded ever so slightly, almost like a small child having a temper tantrum.

"How long have you been buying prostitutes?" He glared at me as he said this.

I was taken by surprise. "I'm sorry. I think you have the wrong person."

"I don't have the wrong person. I want to know about the hookers you ordered from Mo'ak."

I didn't know what to say. "I didn't order any prostitutes. I'm not sure what you're referring to."

My conversation counterpart twisted his head and popped his neck. "How long have you known Jedediah Stark?" Things were starting to come together.

"You mean Captain Stark? From the Damascus?"

"Don't play games with me, yes I mean Captain Stark from the Damascus. I saw you having dinner with him yesterday evening. I suppose you're going to tell me that you weren't buying prostitutes from him."

The conversation was beginning to make me very uncomfortable. "I wasn't looking for prostitutes; I was just looking for a ride to the next space port."

The fat-jowled man laughed at that. "You were looking for a ride on a freighter? If you want me to buy your lies, you're going to have to come up with something much better than that!"

I told you that I might not know who I am, but I know who I was. I might not be proud of some of the things I was, but right now my refugee skills were going to have to save me. "What evidence am I being held on?"

My counterpart leaned forward in his chair. "The evidence that you were conspiring to buy goods from Captain Stark. I have witnesses."

"That's hardly evidence." I was able to turn out that part of my personality with relative ease and put the intimidation back in his lap. "You saw us talking but as far as you know, we were discussing the price of tea in China. Now, if I'm not being held on evidence I demand you let me go!"

"On whose authority?"

"You don't need authority if you have no reason to hold me!"

"I have all the authority in the universe. You're going to see the magistrate!"

It was about an hour later I was taken to see the judge on the space station. My so called insubordination with the Transit Authority had bought me a black eye and a bloody nose, but I've had far worse. The judge resided in a small office and to my surprise; Captain Stark and Jenna were in there also. Things were starting to get interesting.

The magistrate read his docket and spoke up. "You three are accused of conspiring of personal trafficking. How do you plead?

It was unanimous. We all said "not guilty" in harmony.

The magistrate didn't even look up from his docket. "There were witnesses that saw you conspiring in an eatery last night and I believe the Damascus was reported loading a group of young ladies of the night at its last stop on Mo'ak. Do you dispute this evidence?"

There was a palpable silence. My mouth gets me in trouble frequently, as evidenced by my black eye, but I had to speak up. "Did you search Captain Stark's ship?"

He finally looked up. Space port magistrates weren't used to being questioned. "Excuse me?"

"I know the Transit Authority searched Captain Stark's ship. No evidence was found of wrong doing, or else these fine people would already be in prison and not subject to the authority of a magistrate. As for me, I'm just a wandering spirit going wherever the road may take me. If you'll review your security cameras, you'll find that I finished Captain Stark's meal when he left the table. If I had money to buy young ladies from Mo'ak, I would surely have money to buy my own food."

"That's hardly a defence."

"How about this? You place three people into a penal colony without a shred of hard evidence and this port furthers its reputation as one being hostile to traders. Your visits and commerce are already down. Other freight captains will no doubt talk and I know how you business types hate that."

Sometimes it's all about speaking the language.

The magistrate, obviously perturbed, stamped three dockets and said, "You're all free to go." Halleluiah, the lord must have been standing by my side on that one.

Outside of the magistrate office, I brushed myself off and looked at Captain Stark. He was shorter than I, but very intimidating. "It seems you need fresh crew."

He began to walk away from me. "I don't need new crew. I have a few left."

"I'm registered."

He kept walking, Jenna was not far behind.

"You owe me one!" That stopped him dead in his tracks.

He turned and walked back to where I was standing, his feet heavy on the ground. "Do you know how to read a cargo manifest?"

"No, but I'm a fast learner."

He stood there looking and not saying anything for a moment.

Finally. "Let's go. I'll get you some quarters. I want to be out of here as soon as possible."

And that, my friends, is how I found my way onto the Damascus.

2

I grew up on a planet called Earth in a little community called Brantley, Florida. My mother was such a wonderful angel. I guess all mothers are in the eyes of babes. Now that I know the kinds of things my parents engaged in, I can't say that I'm especially proud of them; but when I was a young man you could never have convinced me that she had ever done any wrong. One thing I remember most from my childhood was a book of Grimm's Fairy Tales. It was a large collection of stories from my planet's history that usually had some sort of lesson attached to it. There was one in particular, however, that really made an impression on me as a boy. In fact, it gave me nightmares for many years. It was the tale of the willful child.

You see, once there was this little boy who was very willful and he never did what his parents asked. After a while, God became displeased with him and let him become very ill. Every doctor in the land tried to help him, but they could not. Their medicine just could not make him better. So, the little boy died and his family lowered him into a grave. They began to spread dirt across him and his little arm reached upward out of the ground. They pushed it back down and covered it again with dirt, but it was of no use. The little arm burst forth again and reached up out of the ground. Then, the mother came forth with a strap and beat the little arm, but it would not yield. Day and night she spanked the little arm until finally; it went down into the ground and stayed there. Even though I knew this lesson, it never stopped me from blazing my own path. Even sometimes when it seemed I was covered in dirt, I still had the undying urge to push my arm out, even though I knew it would be strapped.

***

The Damascus was an old grandfather of a ship on the outside, and the inside was no better. Strictly a utility vessel, nothing here was made for aesthetics or comfort. There were four cargo bays, every one about the size of a basketball court. Each one had its own separate climate control and bay doors. They were completely separate units, accessible by a long elevated walkway from the cockpit or hallways aligning the engine room in the center. The crew quarters and common room were located directly under the cockpit and the galley. I tell you, comfort was not designed into the vessel. My assigned space actually had two bunks in it, but I was the only one there which suited me just fine. The room, if you could call it that, was not much larger than my prison cell was all those years ago. The difference, I had to tell myself, was that I could come and go as I wished.

Understanding a manifest wasn't too hard and it didn't take long to learn. I had to inventory the freight and make sure it was secured properly. In bay three, I had to make sure the climate controls were adjusted according to the required specifications. It was filled with some sort of medical equipment we were taking to Alpha Centauri station. Two of the other bays were full of various crates and containers, ready to be brought to whoever was on the other side of the order.

That hot shot pilot I told you about before? It was Jenna! I had never heard of a woman who flew freight before, much less an Inillian. Most cargo pilots were big burly men that would just as soon pound you in to the ground as give you the time of day. Pilots with her skills usually flew shuttles and jets, but there she was on the Damascus. Her appearance didn't seem to fit, but her personality did. She always seemed to have something better to do than be sociable.

The first evening we left dock she came knocking at my door. I had been reading from the book of Psalms. I tucked my Bible up under my mattress before I opened up, I didn't want it to be found. The back cover had been torn off a year before and I had to be careful to not rip the pages. They were so thin and delicate. Jenna's fur had turned into an easy brown. I was sure her emotions would be easy to read as her coat changed color with each one, but I didn't really know what any of her many hues meant yet. Aside from the fur, Inillians had hair on their head, too; just like humans. It also changed color to match the fur. Jenna's was shoulder length and straight, almost covering her left eye. Her hair had been tied back at the port; I hadn't seen it down before. Needless to say she was striking. Her eyes were a deep green that caught your gaze and didn't want to let go.

"Is the freight down?"

"I beg your pardon?"

She shifted her weight from one foot to the next and sighed. "Is all of the cargo secured to the floor?"

"Oh, yes. I made sure of that."

"And you did your double checks? I'm about to engage the cruise engines and I don't need loose materials bouncing around in the bays."

"Yes, ma'am. I did everything Captain Stark showed me." I smiled at her, trying to lighten the mood.

"Show me your manifest." It was going to take a while to earn her trust.

I gave her my tablet indicating my double checks tying every last piece of equipment to the floor clamps. She almost seemed to lighten up to a dark yellow as she read over it.

She thrust my tablet back at me and said, "Very well. We'll be going to cruise momentarily; I suggest you strap yourself in."

Going to cruise was rough, but once you got there it was smooth sailing.

The next morning I went to bay four, which was the empty one, so I could learn more about the climate controls without putting the cargo at risk. The temperature control was pretty cut and dry, but the humidity settings were a bit more complex. They were tied into the thermostat with some kind of protocol that I couldn't quite grasp, but it was coming to me. In every bay there was this one dial located under a plastic box that I wasn't quite sure about. It was unlabeled except for little hash marks going in a circle. There was only one way to tell what this did, I turned it.

If you've never been on a starship, you don't know about the residual hum. It was there all the time, a sound made by the engines. It wasn't a great nuisance; your body had a way of tuning it out after a couple of days. When I turned this dial, I suddenly became aware of the hum growing much louder. The next thing I noticed was my knees getting weaker. I thought I was having a stroke, but then I realized it was a self contained artificial gravity module. I quickly turned it back to where it was. The hum went away and my legs grew all of their strength back!

Without warning, a voice boomed from the upper walkway. It startled me with my newly refreshed ears and I nearly jumped out of my skin. It was Captain Stark. "Stop that!"

"I was just familiarizing myself with the environmental controls."

He hurried down the steps to where I was standing. "Gravity setting is *not* an environmental control."

"I'm sorry. I didn't know. I was just trying to learn the ship."

The captain seemed perturbed. "You don't need to learn this ship. Listen, I'll carry you through three more space docks, and then my debt to you is repaid. We're done."

I wasn't sure how to respond to that. "Alright, just please talk to me before you drop me off at some random port."

"Okay, but don't touch anything if I haven't shown it to you."

"Yes sir."

That was pretty much my experience with the rest of the crew. They really didn't communicate with me. The cook brought me my meals to my quarters; I didn't eat with the staff. There were times I would walk through the common room and all conversation would stop until I left out the other side. It wasn't that I wasn't a member of their crew; it was that I wasn't a freight worker. Oh, I had a freight registration with the Transit Authority, but that didn't mean much to those folks. They had spent untold years flying cargo from one end of the galaxy to the other and if you hadn't lived the same lifestyle, then you were an outsider. It was as simple as that.

The first two days at Alpha Centauri station were very busy and hectic. We unloaded the medical supplies and some containers out of bay two and took on a load of mining equipment bound for a distant colony on the other side of Betelgeuse. I say we, but it was mostly me loading and unloading. I could really start to feel my age. My old body wasn't used to that type of hard manual labor. It took me longer than it should have, but I got done what I needed to get done. All four bays were packed to the brim and I had the long and tedious task of inventory before we launched. It was a welcome relief from the heavy labor.

The freighters that went into deep space usually had a cook. Most of the time they were just a crewman assigned to do the cooking rather than a true culinary artist. I've heard that they would draw lots before taking off to see who would have to prepare the food with each mission. David Jessup was a tall and slender man who cooked full time and actually seemed to enjoy it.

He came to me while I was inventorying bay two and handed me a pad. "I need these items moved up to the galley tonight."

I looked at the list and surprised myself that I remembered where some of the items were. "Y'all are no doubt taking advantage of my free labor, here; aren't you?"

He grew a large self satisfied grin that seemed to extend from ear to ear. "Yep, Captain Stark has given us permission to delegate any tasks to you!"

"Lovely. I have lots of freight to inventory; it may be tomorrow morning before I can get this to you."

David closed his eyes and shook his head. His nose almost seemed too large for his face and it looked comical seeing him do this. "No good, I need this tonight. We're all going on shore leave since you're taking so long and I have to have this stuff in the galley when I get back."

"You're all leaving?"

"What's wrong? Afraid to be here by yourself?"

"No, I just didn't think ya'll would trust me enough to watch the ship by myself."

He laughed out loud at that. "We don't! Jenna and Captain stark have the keys. You won't be able to leave this ship or take off with it even if you wanted to!" He walked away laughing and shaking his head.

It was not going to be an easy job.

After taking the crates up to the galley, my arms felt like wet noodles. I needed to take a break. It only took a little time of idleness before my curiosity got the better of me. I hadn't really been to the upper deck except for when Captain Stark had showed me around and then told me I was not welcome up there. The galley was on the port side of the ship and a

27

dining hall was located just past the hallway on the starboard. On the bow end (that's the front for you land based folk), was the cockpit. It was locked up tighter than a solitary confinement ward.

As the short hallway went further back a ways, it teed off and there were doors that lead to the upper walkways of the cargo bays. In between the two rows of bays was the engine room, it spanned two decks and it was locked up tight, also. They sure didn't plan on letting me get anywhere close to anything sensitive on this ship.

Enough exploring, I had work to do.

I went back to bay four; there was a fresh load and lots of paperwork that went with it. The room was terribly quiet. I was so used to the residual hum that I missed it when it was gone. Every sound I made seemed to echo in the mostly filled chamber. My hearing had always been very good, that's part of the reason I was able to pick up the guitar so quickly. I loved sound, but I respected silence. The absence of noise always seemed to make it easier to get closer to God.

I took a moment to pray since no one was around. It seemed like a good time.

In the still of the stockroom, I thought I heard voices. Whispering voices. Maybe one of the crew had stayed behind. I called out, "Is anyone here?" The voices stopped.

I thought maybe I was just getting old, hearing things. I read somewhere that people could start hearing voices if they were alone for long periods of time. I was lonely, but on the ship I was far from being alone. I went about my work and didn't give it a second thought. Until I heard it again.

Now, the first time I wasn't sure if it was my imagination or not. The second time, I know I heard someone talking. It was coming from the bow end of the cargo bay. I thought I was alone on the ship. I had been all over the upper deck and what wasn't opened had been secured from the outside. The same with the crew quarters below, all locked from the outside. There was no way any one of the crew had remained on board.

There it was again, a whisper; a loud whisper. I couldn't tell if it was male or female, but it was definitely a whisper. I called out again "Who is that?"

Silence.

Quiet.

I wasn't far from the bow wall, so I made my way to it and placed my head against the metal panel there. It was cold against my ear. Patiently, I listened.

I was so engrossed in listening for voices that I didn't hear the footsteps coming into the bay. When my visitor spoke, I jumped and yelped a little. Just a little.

"Who are you?" It was an inspector for the Transit Authority. He was wearing the typical blue jumpsuit they wore with his institutions patch on the left breast and right sleeve. It was a circle, a triangle and a square laid on top of one another. It was supposed to be a symbol of cooperation, but it had become a heavily loathed image amongst traders. He had a small electronic data pad and one hand and the other was resting on the barrel of his rifle. A strap kept it secure about his shoulders.

"I'm Jacob Mozel. I work here. I didn't think inspectors were supposed to come aboard without the crew present." This was starting to make me uncomfortable.

"You're present and I'm making an inspection, so that makes it official."

"Yeah, but it seems you didn't know I was here before you came into the room." Maybe I shouldn't have said that, but I was always a willful child.

His hand moved from the barrel of his gun to the grip. "Is that your cargo manifest?"

I nodded and handed it to him. I sure didn't want to escalate things at that point.

He reviewed it carefully. Without looking up, he asked a question. "Are you carrying anything from Mo'ak?"

I started to have an idea about where this was going.

A voice. The same whisper from before. It was faint and unintelligible, but it was a voice nonetheless.

My Transit Authority friend looked up startled. "What was that?"

I knew that if I didn't play my cards right this could end badly. "What was what?"

"Don't play games with me. I heard something. It came from behind that wall."

He walked over to the panel I had been listening to when he came in and placed his ear against it. "What's behind this panel?"

I swallowed. I didn't know what was there, but I had a pretty good idea I didn't want him to find out. "A fuel cell I think. I don't know."

He placed his data pad in a pocket and pulled his rifle into position, pointing at me. "Why did you have your head against that wall?"

"I have an earache that hurts terribly and the metal is cool against my skin." My mind was racing trying to keep with this conversation.

"Open the panel."

"I don't know how."

He pulled out his data pad again, pushed a button and spoke into it. "This is Marcus. I think I have something on The Damascus in the fourth cargo bay. I'm requesting back up."

The situation was going from bad to worse. Marcus holstered his pad once again and pointed to the wall with the barrel of his gun.

"I'm telling you, I don't know how. We really should call Captain Stark."

That idea got shut down real quick. He made me kneel down on my knees, put my hands behind my back and he placed me in a pair of plasticuffs. He then proceeded to run his hands all along the wall, seemingly looking for a way to remove the panel.

The Transit Authority must train their men well, because it only took him a few minutes to find a lever that I didn't even know was there. He pushed it in and a pair of large handles came out of the wall. The panel came out easily on tracks and slid to one side. Behind it was a well lit room. I think I was more surprised than he was.

He poked his head in, looking left and the right before entering. Through the door, I could see the corner of a bunk suspended against the wall with a sheet hanging off of one side. It all suddenly made sense. I didn't know what to do, but the Mo'ak prostitutes did.

Four of them jumped on Marcus before he had a chance to react. He stumbled back a few steps and fell to the ground with a heavy thud. More girls came from the room. Most just stood there in disbelief, but two jumped on him and held him down while the others clawed at his face like wild animals.

The cuffs were tight on my wrists; there was no way I would be able to pull out of them. Not every skill I learned as a criminal was a good skill, but they would come in to play now. I quickly rolled over and tried to push my hands down under my butt to at least get my arms in front. My shoulders were exhausted from working all day and my bones weren't what they used to be, but I was making progress.

Rivulets of crimson were forming on the Transit Authority worker's face as he pushed the girls off one by one and managed to rise to a standing position, however hunched over. The Mo'ak girls looked just like humans, except they were slender and much shorter. Marcus had no problem pushing them away. He tried to wipe his eyes with his sleeve and yelled out.

I almost had my arms free.

Three of the girls lunged at him and one jumped up on his shoulders. He spun in a half circle and threw the one off of his trunk, but the other girls were clawing him mercilessly. I watched in horror as Marcus wrapped both of his hands around one dainty neck and squeezed. He lifted the little girl up into the air, his thick fingers choking the life out of her. She tried to pry his hands loose, but she couldn't get a grip. Her small body flailed in the air, dangling above the ground.

"Stop it! Stop it!" I yelled out. He didn't seem to hear me. My shoulders were on fire and my wrists felt like they were almost around my bottom, but they wouldn't budge.

Just then, the little Mo'ak girl landed a kick between Marcus's legs. He screamed, stumbled and then went down to his knees; but he never loosened his grip.

Another one of the girls jumped onto his back and began pummeling him with everything she had, which wasn't much more than pure spirit. Marcus fell forward into the secret room, smashing the back of the little girls head on the ground. I heard the unmistakable crunch of skull colliding with steel.

I flew into a rage. So many times I've ask for the Lord's serenity, so many times I've asked Him to not let the fury in my heart come to surface. But God knew I was a willful child. Just as he knew it when I killed my own father.

I finally managed to pull my wrists around my butt and out from under my feet. I jumped up and ran to where Marcus was. He still had his hands gripped around the girl's neck, but he was repeatedly slamming her head against the floor. A large puddle of blood was pooling there and growing larger with each crunch of bone on steel.

I couldn't tell if there was any life left in this little girl's eyes, but I knew I had to do something. I pushed my wrists down around Marcus's face and pulled my plasticuffs tight around his neck. I yanked him back and he finally let go of the little girl. He was shorter than me, so it didn't take much effort for me to raise him into the air and step backwards. His legs were flailing, kicking at nothing.

His fingers started to pull at the cuffs around his neck as he gagged. His nails, ripping at his own flesh trying to remove my tourniquet.

I saw something out of the corner of my eye then. One of the girls had grabbed the Transit Authority rifle, cocked it and put the barrel against Marcus's head.

God please forgive me. I nodded and told her to do it.

The rifle discharged without much of a sound, but bits of flesh and blood sprayed across the cargo bay. I dropped Marcus to floor and we all stood there in horror, looking at what we had done.

It was self defense. I had to save that girl, I know that now. But I just don't know if that made it right.

I heard voices coming from the hallway. "Which bay was he in?"

"I don't remember; we'll have to search them all."

I looked around at the girls. They were terrified. "Get back in the room; get back in the room, hurry!" I said in an urgent whisper.

The girls scrambled, all except one. She was gone; her eyes were glazed and far away.

I shoved her body up under a bunk so it would be out of sight.

Marcus was still lying in the cargo bay. I grabbed his uniform and drug his body though the open panel. I reached around to the handle and saw three Transit Authority workers enter the cargo bay. I turned to the girls. There were nine of them still alive and they were all huddled into the corner. If I shut the panel now, the men would see us for sure.

"Get under your beds; under the beds and be quiet!" They scrambled and slid up under their bunks.

Marcus's body was still lying out in the open. I shoved it up under the bunk closest to me and climbed up under the bed, lying on top of him. The feeling of a soft dead body underneath me almost made me sick, but I held my food in somehow.

Just next to me and the corpse was one of the girls. She had just enough time to see me and the cadaver shove up next to her and her eyes grew wide. She opened her mouth to scream, but I clamped my hand over it. I leaned over and whispered in her ear. "Don't make a sound. Don't make a whimper."

I knew the men would come around the cargo any second and see the blood there; I said a quiet prayer that they would not find us.

We could hear the boots of the Transit Authority security team walking through the cargo hold. *Any second*, I thought. *Any second, they'll see the blood and then God help me I don't know what else to do.*

The little girl started shaking her head.

I said to her, "Listen to my voice, only the sound of my voice, nothing else."

I could see by the look in her eyes that she was hearing what I was saying, but I was not confident enough to let go of her mouth.

I whispered into her ear. "The Lord is my shepherd; I shall not want."

I could hear the boots coming around the corner.

"He maketh me to lie down in green pastures: he leadeth me beside the still waters."

The boots entered the room, there were three men. I could see them walking right by us.

"He restoreth my soul: he leadeth me in the paths of righteousness for his name's sake."

They tracked through the blood, leaving footprints as they went. How could they not see it?

"Yea, though I walk through the valley of the shadow of death, I will fear no evil: for thou art with me; thy rod and thy staff they comfort me."

One of the Transit Authority workers spoke up "I don't see anything. Where is Marcus? Are you sure he radioed from this ship?"

"Thou preparest a table before me in the presence of mine enemies: thou anointest my head with oil; my cup runneth over."

"I don't see anything either. He should have stayed at his post if he called in trouble. We're going to have to make a report to the major. I sure hope this ship hasn't planned on leaving for a while."

"Surely goodness and mercy shall follow me all the days of my life: and I will dwell in the house of the Lord forever."

The boots walked out. We stayed there for at least five minutes before we dared move.

The pools of blood on the floor had already begun to dry into a darker red. There was no covering it up.

***

I walked back into the cargo bay to see Jenna standing there, frozen; staring at the mess. Her green eyes were saucers in her little cat face and her hand was over her mouth, covering a silent scream. The fur that had been an easy tan just a few days ago had changed into a ghastly white.

Captain Stark ran around the corner, a vein was already starting to bulge on his bald head. "What did you do? What did you do?" He shoved me up against the wall and a fine sheen of sweat was already beading up on his temples.

Out of the frying pan and into the fire.

3

I once read somewhere that a philosopher said "Justice is contingent upon the individual. A justice *system* is a compact between said individuals." I can't remember who said that quote, but it was coming to mind as I was standing there with Captain Stark's anger to my throat. I had just killed a Transit Authority officer and placed him and his crew in mortal danger. I said a silent prayer and asked that God be the one to judge me regardless of this man's justice.

He pressed his forearm up against my neck, pinning my back against the wall and causing me to gag. Instinctively, I wrapped both hands around his arm, trying to free myself, but it was of no use. He was strong. He yelled in my face, "Did you kill that agent?" His breath was stinking of garlic and rotten teeth. It was all I could do to not lose my groceries right then and there.

I wasn't sure what to say. I'm sure my eyes were as wide as a rabbit in a trap. For the second time in as many hours, one of the Mo'ak girls stepped in with a move that relieved me of the burden of decision. It was the one who had fired the gun. "No, I killed him." She was much more cool and collected than I was at the moment. "The bad man was killing Sarah. That one [she pointed at me] was trying to save her but I'm the one that killed him!"

The young prostitute might have spoken up for me; but in an ironic twist, it was the Transit Authority that saved me.

James Jessup was the ships mechanic. He was a monster of a man with hands as large as a bear's claws and a brown beard that grew down to his chest. He ran into the room, slightly short of breath. If he was fazed at all by the scene before him, he didn't show it. "Captain, the Transit Authority's at the aft hatch. They want in."

Stark released my throat much to the delight of my lungs and looked around for a second. I could almost see him regain his composure like a fisherman reeling in a net.

Awkward silence.

"Jenna, warm up the engines." The captain didn't even make eye contact with her.

He was deep inside his mind; it was running as fast as it could right now.

Jenna was still standing there, white as death with her hand over her mouth. She seemed not to hear him.

"Jenna!"

That caught her attention.

"Yes, Captain."

Stark turned a gaze on her that said he was in charge. He never raised his voice to her, he didn't have to. "I said, warm up the engines. Now."

Lines of light blue rippled through her pale fur as she leapt away from the cargo bay.

Captain Stark and James walked back towards the aft hatch. I didn't know where else to go, so I followed. The mechanic activated a small monitor by the hatch. I could see a man in a Transit Authority jumpsuit with a gold rope around his left shoulder. I didn't know what kind of rank this indicated, but I knew it was more than just a grunt. "Captain Stark?"

"Yes?"

"I'm General Sanders, the CO here at Alpha Centauri. We're missing a soldier. I need to come aboard. "

"Your soldier's not here, General."

"Just the same, his last transmission was from your cargo bay. I need to come aboard."

"Are you telling me that your man came on my ship without my crew present?"

"I'm telling you that since you're here, I don't need your permission to do an inspection. You can either open the door for us, or we'll force it open."

The captain turned off the monitor and shot a quick glance at his mechanic. His next two words would define the rest of our lives together. "Strap in."

No sooner had he said it than a loud clang came from the hatch. They were loosening up the door with a ram. The next step would be plasma torches.

Stark wasted no time. He and James had already begun running down the corridor towards the bow when the ram hit. I was frozen, but the second clank broke me out of my stupor and I followed not far behind. I could hear the captain yelling as he ran. "Jenna! Jenna! Go now!"

I ran and climbed the steps to the upper deck as fast as my old bones would carry me. The door to the cockpit was open and it was only the second time I'd seen inside it. The ship lurched as I scurried through the door. I held my own, but it was enough to throw James to the floor, he was more out of breath than I was.

There were two large bucket seats in the front. On the port side, Jenna was managing a console and pushing furiously on a well worn yoke. I couldn't see her face, but her coat had changed to a deep scarlet. Stark was just strapping in the starboard seat next to her. David was already secure in one of the four aft chairs, his face pale and sweat dripping from his chin. James righted himself and climbed into one of the oversized seats. I did the same just before the ship lurched again.

I heard another clang from the aft hatch, it almost sounded as if something broke it open. The captain was furious. "Damnit, get us out of here!"

Jenna matched his tone. "I'm trying! The docking clamps are still attached!"

"Break 'em!"

"I'm trying!"

Jenna pushed hard on the yoke and the ship lurched forward again. I could feel something tearing loose by the way it was moving. We turned to the left and I would have fallen out of my seat had I not been belted in. Crashes of untold amounts of cargo resounded throughout the ship as unsecured merchandise fell to one side.

With a final pull, we broke loose and the Damascus lumbered into space.

Another awkward silence.

James was the first one to speak, "did we get away?"

Without looking back, it was Jenna that answered his question. "No! We've got three guard ships hot on our tail!" A monitor popped up in the front console and we could see them there, closing fast.

chunk chunk chunk chunk chunk

I knew what it was, but the question needed to be asked. "What's that?"

The captain answered "We're taking fire!"

"Hold on!" Jenna yelled and jerked her yoke to the left. I felt myself grow heavy in my seat as the giant ship banked. The crashes of cargo being flung about the bays came again, louder than before.

chunk chunk chunk chunk chunk

"Get us out of here!" David screamed from his seat.

"This ship wasn't built for speed!" Jenna yelled back. "I'm powering up the cruise engines now. Thirty seconds!"

chunk chunk chunk chunk chunk

The sound of bullets against the hull was sickening and my heart leapt up into my chest every time I heard it. Jenna banked right and yelled at the captain. "Do it now! Do it now!"

Stark grabbed onto a double throttle on the center console and pushed it forward. The sound of cruise engines powering up filled the cockpit and then something happened. It almost sound like a balloon popping and then a loud hiss. The engines stopped. "What happened?" I was starting to panic.

Jenna was reviewing a panel of dials and monitors way beyond my comprehension. "One of those bullets punched a hole in a starboard manifold! We're leaking coolant!"

The captain swivelled around in his chair and stopped, facing his mechanic. "Can you fix it?"

"I can bypass it!"

chunk chunk chunk chunk chunk

"Do it!"

James unbelted and rose up out of his chair. I knew he had a job to do and I knew our lives depended on him doing it quick, but three seconds wouldn't hurt. I grabbed the man by his wrist as he walked past. He glanced down at me, a very intimidating figure. "Go with the Father, the Son and the Holy Ghost, amen." Without a response, he disappeared out of the back of the cockpit with a speed that was surprising for a man his size.

Another burst of bullets hit.

"We're losing pressure in bay one!" I don't really recall who said that, but I do remember it.

Just then, James's voice came over a speaker. "I'm bypassing the coolant leak, but three of the cruise engines are down!"

It was Stark's turn to lose the color in his face. "Can we get out of here with only one engine?"

chunk chunk chunk chunk chunk

Jenna turned the massive ship again. She was starting to look tired. "I don't think so, we're pretty heavy."

I could see the muscles in the captain's jaws as they clenched. He took a deep breath and exhaled slowly. I thought he was about to give up, but I had underestimated him. "I'm opening the doors in bays one and two."

Jenna turned to him astonished, "Captain?" A ripple of blonde flecked across her red fur. It made an uneasy contrast.

"I'm doing it! Hold on!" He set to mashing a series of buttons and a klaxon sounded with a red light on the ceiling.

The entire ship shook and jumped as the bays suddenly depressurized and tons of freight collided with itself and was flung out into open space. The resulting rumble was like the most powerful thunderstorm I had ever heard.

chunk chunk chunk chunk chunk

We were still taking fire from the guard ships. Captain Stark grabbed the yoke on his side of the ship and pushed it hard to the right. The force made my entire body slump to one side. I was going to vomit if we did much more of that. David didn't appear any more well off than I did.

"What are you doing?" Jenna's voice reverberated through the cockpit.

"Unload bay three on my mark!"

"What?"

"Empty bay three on my mark!" I could feel the Damascus circling around in space.

Suddenly, the guard ships were in front of us. Then they disappeared from the opposite side of the windshield.

"Mark!"

Jenna slammed her hand down hard on a button and a klaxon sounded as before. The same rattle of rustling cargo filled the ship but it was much quicker this time. It suddenly dawned on me what the captain was doing.

I trained my eyes on the aft monitor just in time to see two of the small cruise ships taken out by large metal crates almost as large as they were. One of them lit up for a second and blew into a million pieces. The other stalled and stopped, dead in its tracks. Pieces of flotsam and jetsam filled the space behind us.

chunk chunk chunk chunk chunk

There was one more ship in pursuit and it was still firing on us. Stark looked over at his pilot. "No more fancy flying. This ship can't take anymore. Straight line, we *have* to outrun them."

Jenna had one hand on the yoke and the other on the left cruise throttle. She jammed it forward and I could hear the one last engine powering up. It sounded anemic without its three brothers.

I could tell something was wrong. We weren't going. "We're still too heavy!"

"I'm going to have to empty bay four! It's the only way!"

My heart raced. I reached over and put my hand on the captain's shoulder. "The girls! You can't! The girls are in there!"

"The girls' quarters are tied in to other systems. As long as they went to their room and strapped in, they'll be alright!" With that he pushed the button. I didn't hear him whisper over the cacophony, but I could see his lips moving. *I hope they went to their room and strapped in.* The klaxon sounded as before, but then something went wrong. A loud scream of metal on metal filled the ship and it ended in a resounding thump.

David was panicking now. "What was that? What was that?"

Captain Stark checked a monitor that was out of my line of sight and then beat the dash with a fist. The cruise engine was screaming louder. I don't know if he was yelling because he was angry or scared or just trying to be heard. It was probably a combination of all three. "The bay didn't empty! All the stuff in it is pushed up against the back wall! We're moving too fast for a vacuum to suck it all out!"

chunk chunk chunk chunk chunk

Jenna was crying. "I can't slow down; they're right on top of us!"

The howl of the single cruise engine was growing louder. Stark yelled again, this time just to be heard over the whine. "The only way to get it out is to shut off the artificial gravity!"

Jenna was pushing on the throttle though it would go no further. "That'll kill the girls!"

The captain started unbuckling his belt. "Then we'll have to go get them. Repressurize the bay!" He turned to David who was panting. "You're with me!"

"I can't! I can't do it!"

"You have to!"

David leaned over to one side and unloaded the contents of his stomach onto the floor. He might have been a good chef, but this business didn't sit well with him.

Stark turned to me, the whites of his eyes were dark red. "You're with me."

I nodded, unbuckled and rose to the task, no matter what it was. I placed my hand on his shoulder, nodded my head and said "God be with us, that's all I have time for. Amen."

He pulled away from my grip and was down the hall before I could get the last words out of my mouth. I followed close behind.

We flew down the steps to the lower deck and made our way to the bay four door. A green light was on indicating that it was already pressurized. We ran in and made our way to the hatch. All of the cargo was piled against the aft wall, making an unorganized pile of junk. Marcus's dead body lay on top of the heap, lifeless and limp.

The captain opened the hatch and told the girls to unstrap and hurry. I ran inside the room to help. One by one, they got loose and followed him out. The last girl was free and running, I brought up the rear. The entire ship was starting to shake under the stress of the one engine. We were making our way towards the door and I could see Stark by the control panel, already starting to turn off the gravity. My legs were getting light as I urged the girls to run as fast as they could.

chunk chunk chunk chunk chunk
chunk chunk chunk chunk chunk

Pieces of metal were flying all across the bay as bullets tore through the hull. A hiss resounded as the air was sucked out of the ship in tiny holes on the wall. If it wasn't for the cry of the overtaxed engines, it would have been deafening. As it was, it whistled just under the surface.

My feet suddenly lost traction and in the low gravity, me and one of the girls began to slide in the wrong direction. I could see Captain Stark in the hallway outside of the bay. He turned his head and yelled towards the cockpit. "You can't bank at this speed!"

Jenna either didn't hear him or she didn't care. This massive ship was banking with a cruise engine engaged!

The gravity went away completely and I felt my body rise into the air. I reached out for the girl that was floating next to me, but I couldn't reach her. My fingertips touched hers, but it just wasn't enough to keep her from floating away. She was screaming and panic filled her face as she drifted off. Weightless, her body was flung to the other end of the bay.

All of the cargo was rising into the air and started to fly about the room. Metal shipping containers, some as large as trucks, took flight and began banging into each other, ricocheting with loud clangs that I felt rather than heard. I was hit by a large crate that slammed into my side. Old ribs crunched and the breath was knocked out of me. Helpless as a leaf in a tornado, I reached out to grab for anything I could as I careened towards the ceiling. I managed to catch myself on the railing of the upper walkway before I hit the roof. Once I stabilized myself, I immediately turned my attention towards the girl. I looked her way just in time to see a barrel impact her and throw her against a far wall. Her mouth was open with a terrifying scream, but I couldn't hear her. Sarah's dead body flew past, limp like a rag doll and blood oozing from her in all directions. She saw that and I could see in her face that she was beyond helping herself. I had to do something. The girl was only twenty feet away from me, but she might as well have been on the other side of the galaxy. Pieces of cargo whipped about the bay in the weightlessness of space. I was going to have to go through that to get to her. There was no way I could just leave and I had only seconds before all of the air was gone and the Captain would have to open the cargo bay.

I closed my eyes and prayed. "God, please show me the way."

When I opened them, there it was. The junk swirling about the room parted and I could see her. A clear path to her! I pushed off with my legs and sailed across the room until I hit the far wall. She was in a state of panic. There was no way she was going to hear what I was going to say. Our gap was still open, but it was closing fast. I grabbed her, held her close, shut my eyes and pushed off towards the door.

I'm not sure who grabbed us and pulled us in, but it felt like a thousand hands all over my entire body. We fell to the floor in the hallway together and I looked up just in time to see the captain close the hatch and empty the bay. The colliding of cargo sounded less and less as it was all sucked out into the vacuum of space. The one remaining engine finally caught traction with the lower weight and the ship took off. We were thrown to the back of the hallway in a tangled mass of angry captain, worn out preacher and frightened Mo'ak pleasure girls; but we were alive. There was no more gunfire.

When we found our feet, Stark took us all up to the galley were the girls could ride in relative safety and I followed him back to the bridge. James had returned to his seat, a deep red spot adorned the side of his face. That would be a black eye the next day.

Jenna jumped up from her seat and embraced the captain. Her fur was slowly fading to a lush shade of green. "We outran them. We're safe."

Captain Stark reached around and reluctantly patted her on the shoulder. I could tell he was not comfortable showing affection. "We outran them. But we're far from safe. We need to set coordinates."

Jenna appeared puzzled as the obvious question graced her cleft lip. "Where do we go?"

The captain ran a hand across his bald head. "The only place we can go. Sanctuary."

Oh no. Not Sanctuary. I think I would have rather taken my chances with the Transit Authority.

4

There was a county fair that came to Brantley every fall. It was full of carnival rides and games of skill, managed by people who always looked like they had seen better days. Of the few that still had teeth, even fewer smelled like they had taken a bath in recent days. But, as a kid, you never really saw the people at a fair. You saw the lights and heard the sounds of bells and whistles and the laughter of the other children as they were spun around and around by rickety midway rides. My mother took me every year. We didn't have much money, but we'd walk down to the fairgrounds and Mother would find a little bit of money to give me and I wouldn't see her until the end of the day when one of the dirty carnies would drive us home. Their cars always stank and they smoked in them, but it was a ride.

There was always this one game at the fair that ended up taking most of my money. It was a basketball throw. Now, if there was one thing I loved more than a carnival, it was basketball. Every year, I told myself that I was bigger and stronger and that I would win the large prize. All I had to do was throw the ball into the hoop! I practiced and practiced with a net I made from an old laundry basket and a ball that a church had brought to me one year. My skills at home got better, but I could never win that prize. I never really wanted a stuffed animal or anything like that; I was just determined to beat the game.

One year, when I was about thirteen or so, I was just sure that it was the year I was going to make it. I took my money to the basketball booth, plopped it down and wasted most of it missing the score. Throw after throw, I don't remember how many, but it was a lot. Every time, the dirty man at the booth would say something very sympathetic and encourage me to try again. I wanted to get one, just one. The booth attendant smiled his toothless smile and said something like *you can do it, I know you can.* He knew I could do it, I knew I could do it, too.

It was about that time that some strange carnie I had never seen before put his hand on my shoulder, leaned over and whispered in my ear, "hey, come with me. I need to show you something."

When I was a young boy, I was wary of strangers; but when I was a teenager, I was bulletproof. I shudder to think now of what kind of trap I could have fallen into, being so naive, but he wasn't looking for trouble. The carnie at the basketball booth pouted his bottom lip and made a clownish frown. "Hurry back, you're getting better!"

The stranger introduced himself, I don't even remember his name now, and told me he had been watching me for quite some time. Together, we walked around to the side of the game booth and stopped. He pointed up to the baskets and said, "Look. Them hoops, they're ovals. They're not round. It's almost impossible to get a ball in that. You can't see it from the front, but you can from here. They're just taking your money, that game's rigged."

I didn't want to believe him, but he was right. It was right here in front of my eyes. I felt angry, though I didn't know who to feel angry at. "Why are you showing me this?"

He looked me squarely in the eye, like a man; it was the first time in my life anybody had ever done that. "I run the dart board down there. That's a man's game!"

I broke away from him and ran to the carnie running the booth and called him on his farce. The man who had been so nice and encouraging before quickly changed into something mean and ugly. His toothless grin became an edentulous scowl and his eyes almost seemed to shrink into his leathery face with a grimace. His voice was even different. "Shut your trap!"

"What?" I didn't know what I expected, but it wasn't that.

He stepped over the table that stood in front of him and pushed me on the shoulder. "I said shut your trap and get out of here before I shut it for you!" There was nothing more to do but turn and walk away.

I'll never forget how I felt that night. It was just a silly game at a carnival, but it was important to me and now I knew that it was all a lie. Some people were nice and amenable when you had money to give them and they were able to fool you; but when the skin was pulled back and you saw the truth, people became very ugly and I discovered that that's where evil lives. Evil is always your friend until you expose it for what it is, then it will ruin you.

It made me question everything else in my life. Who else lied to me every day and who pretended to be my friend? Unfortunately, I found lies and deception in most places I looked. I guess you could say that was the day that I became angry and I wasn't able to begin to live with myself until way after I had already murdered my father. I didn't have a choice when I killed him; but when it made me feel satisfied, I cried for what I had become.

Why am I telling you this? Partly because I'm an old man and I have a tendency to ramble. Partly because you need to know how I arrived at where I am now and why I made the decisions I made.

***

Sanctuary was visible in the blackness of space from many miles away. It almost blended in with the starry backdrop of the galaxy until the cross came into view. The Illuminated Crucifix stood high atop every harbor of the True Church like a vulture and that one was no exception. As we got closer, the rest of Sanctuary came slowly into view. It was larger than a standard space station, but not quite as big as a trading post. At its center it must have been two miles across, but the top and bottom tapered off in giant cones. The bottom was plain, adorned with nothing more than docking ports, windows and access panels. Strictly utilitarian. The top cone, however, was almost gaudy in its presentation. Lights covered it from base to crucifix; some flashing some chasing, some constantly changing colors. Statues of cherubs and angels were affixed to the golden structure, their trumpets aimed at the deepest, darkest regions of space.

The monitor in the center console of the Damascus rose up again and the face of a young woman wearing a headset came into view. Her smile was too perfect. "Welcome to Sanctuary!"

Captain Stark leaned in towards the monitor. I couldn't see his face, but I don't imagine he was returning her grin. "I need to speak to the bishop."

"Do you have an appointment?"

Jedediah paused and took in a deep breath. He was trying to keep his composure and doing an excellent job under the circumstances.

"No, I don't have an appointment."

The girl on the monitor screen puckered her lips in a condescending fashion. "Ooohhh. You'll need an appointment to see him. I can make you one next Tuesday if you like!" Her demeanor was like syrup.

"I don't have time for these games. I need to speak to the bishop and I need to speak to him now!" The captain yelled in a gradual crescendo until he yelled the last word.

The girl's smile disappeared and she pushed some buttons on a console out of site. "Stand by, sir."

The monitor blinked out and then it came back on a few seconds later, displaying a man with the same fake smile and too perfect hair. "Welcome to Sanctuary!" His teeth seemed too big for his face and they were a fine porcelain white.

Stark was getting more irritated now. He spoke slower and more deliberate. "I need to speak with the bishop."

"Do you have an appointment?"

"No I don't have a blasted appointment!" He was yelling at the top of his lungs now. The captain was a man that was easy to agitate. "I have Transit Authority hot on my tail and unless you want them all over your space in the next few hours, I suggest you let me speak with the bishop right now!"

The man on the monitor was still smiling. "Sir, the Transit Authority has no jurisdiction here. Now, if you want to make an appointment to see the bishop I can make you one for next Tuesday."

Jenna cast a glance at the captain; they had worked together so long they didn't need words to communicate.

"I'm coming in to the open bay on your port. You can tell the bishop that Jedediah Stark is here. He'll see me."

The screen went blank again and Jenna set a course for the open bay, which was already starting to close.

We were no more than eight hundred meters from the bay doors when they reversed their course and started opening again. The monitor blinked once more and a man in bishop's robes appeared on the screen. I knew the face in an instant. That day was just full of moments that went from bad to worse. I swiveled my chair around as quick as I could, facing the rear. I said a silent prayer that the man hadn't caught a glimpse of me. It was inevitable that he would find out I was here, but the captain didn't need that sort of complication right now.

Tamra, the Mo'ak pleasure girl who had fired the gun was poking her head out from the galley and watching the commotion in the cockpit. Her eyes had grown as wide as saucers and her hand was covering her mouth, which was opening and closing without words. I knew the look, it was probably the same one I had on my face. She recognized the bishop and she was terrified of him. We made eye contact just long enough for her to know I knew something was wrong and she ducked back into the galley. I closed my eyes and listened.

"Welcome to Sanctuary, Captain Stark! So nice to see you!"

"I don't have time to make small talk, Barabbas. I need to dock and I need to do it now."

I could hear the smug grin in Bishop Barabbas' voice as he tried to turn on his fake charm. "By all means! Proceed to any port you like and I'll meet you there."

I could feel the large ship move ahead at Jenna's gentle touch and I turned around just in time to see us swallowed whole by giant landing bay doors. We landed as tender as a baby's touch and we all undid our straps. Stark put his hands on Jenna's shoulder. "You're staying with the ship."

Her fur was a soft orange, but it rippled with black. She was not happy with the decision. "You need me with you."

"No, I need you with the ship. You leave at the slightest sign of trouble. We weren't supposed to bring the girls here. I don't know what to expect." She was still seated and he stared her down for a tense moment.

"Okay, but I don't like it."

He patted her shoulder and walked away. "Duly noted."

James was not far behind him. "I've got to take a closer look at that starboard manifold." David left the cockpit without a sound. It was just me, Jenna and the girls left on the upper deck.

The girls! I needed to talk to Tamra!

I hot footed it over to the galley, which was only about ten steps and peered in. Most of the girls had taken off their straps and were pacing about the room. A couple were crying and a few of them were holding and rocking their friends in comfort. Tamra was sitting in a chair, chewing on her fingernail. I grabbed her by the arm and stood her up, not forcefully, but she was frightened enough to do anything anybody told her at this point.

I led her to a cargo bay so we could talk in private. She knew what I wanted, but she wouldn't look me in the eyes. "You know that man." It was more of a statement than a question, but I found myself growing anxious when she wouldn't answer.

"Tell me how you know that man."

She shook her head.

"Tamra, I just saved your life. You and all of your friends. Now, I know that you recognized that man and that you don't like him. I can help you stay safe, but you *have* to talk to me."

She looked up at me and her eyes were moist with tears that hadn't quite spilled out over her eyelids. "I am not a pleasure girl by choice."

I don't know why that surprised me, but it did.

"Me and all the rest. We were taken from our homes in the middle of the night. Men would come, strong men. My father and the people of the village, they would try to fight; but they were outnumbered. The last time I saw my mother, she was fighting the strangers that came into our home. I don't know what happened to her. They took me away, me and all the rest." Her story brought back memories of my own that I had to keep hidden for now.

She took a moment. I gave her all the time she needed, I was in this for the long haul whether I liked it or not. "We were taken to large houses in the cities where we were made to be pleasure girls. He was there, that man."

I was in shock. "He was there? He was at a pleasure house on Mo'ak?"

"No, I mean yes, I mean, he did not use the girls. But, he was there and the house masters, they followed him wherever he went. I saw him go there twice and the house masters always followed him as he came and went. Always. That's all I know, I swear it."

A thought crossed my mind. "How did you come to be on this ship?"

"The captain, he bought us."

"Bought you? He doesn't seem like the type."

"No, he never asked for the pleasure. He only bought us."

"Where is he taking you?"

Her eyes grew blank. "I don't know. He only bought us."

I could tell by the look in her eyes she was telling the truth. A single tear spilled out over her lower eyelid and ran down her cheek. "On Mo'ak, do your people worship a creator?"

"We have many spirits that some believe in. Hundreds."

"I'm going to teach you a prayer that I learned a long time ago. The god of my people can be yours too, if you'll let him."

She nodded her head. "I have seen what your God can do."

We knelt down together. I looked at her and said, "Say what I say."

"Grant me, Oh Lord, Thy protection. And in protection, strength. And in strength, understanding. And in understanding, knowledge. And in knowledge, the knowledge of justice. And in the knowledge of justice, the love of it. And in the love of it, the love of all existences. And in that love, the love of spirit and all creation. Amen."

I took her back to her sisters and retired to my quarters. I reached under my mattress and felt the Bible hiding there. I dare not take it out, not there. There was too much to lose. But, I took great comfort in just knowing it was there. Nothing else to do now but give my trouble to the Lord and wait.

I don't know how long it was, but David was the one to come knocking at my door. "Captain wants everyone up top." I didn't know what was going on, so I followed him.

In the galley, the rest of the crew minus the girls were speaking with Bishop Barabbas. There was no avoiding it now. He saw me, adopted an unreadable look on his face and walked slowly towards me.

"Jacob, my brother, I haven't seen you in so long!" He wrapped his arms around me and I reluctantly returned the semi-affection.

"It's been many years." What to do? All I could think of was to let God handle this one. Barabbas let go of me and stared into my eyes.

"Where did…how…I don't understand. You're on a cargo ship?"

I stepped back. "It's a long story."

Captain Stark stepped in-between us. "Wait, you know each other?"

The bishop was sporting a large grin now. "Know each other? We were roommates in seminary!"

There was a silence.

"You know. No matter what the True Church says, God forgives and he has forgiven you."

It was Jenna's turn to speak up. "Seminary? You're a priest?"

Barabbas cast a long glance at her then back at me. "I see. They don't know."

I could tell this conversation was making Stark very uncomfortable. "Is this something I need to know? We have very pressing matters at hand and I'd like to get on with it so we can get out of here and back to business."

All eyes were on me. I sat down and told them my story, some of it anyway.

"I wasn't always just a drifter. I attended the Seminary of the True Church and after many years of study and piety, I became a priest. It was something God had called me to do. To study his word, to understand it, to bring it where it needed to be."

"And he did!" I was surprised when Barabbas interjected. "Immediately after school he set out to a little system called Santos. A hard place that is."

"Yes, it was a hard place. A group of corporations and mining guilds were trying to teraform the planet and I was sent there with a mission to help with the colonists. I was there about six months before I was recalled. You see, when I entered seminary, I lied about who I was.

"There were all sorts of questions, all sorts of inquiries. They want to know where you were born, where you went to school. I even think they asked what my first word was. I told them everything I could. Everything except that I was a murderer. You see, I stabbed my father in the back with a twelve inch knife. Right through his beating heart and out the other side. I spent twenty years in prison, a third of my life. I knew they would never let me become a priest having been patricidal, so I lied.

"You're all wondering what drives a man to kill his own father. I can see it in your eyes. It was my dear sweet mother, bless her heart. My father was a hard man. He drank like a fish, fought like a wild dog and I shudder to think what else. My childhood was filled with regular beatings. Black eyes, broken fingers. For a long time I thought that was how everybody lived, I never knew any better. As I grew older, I grew tough and mean like he did. I guess we never get too far from our roots. I learned how to drink and cuss and fight from my old man. He taught me bitterness, because that was all he ever knew and I presume that's all his father had ever taught him.

"Well, it came to pass one day when I was about fifteen that he was in one of his usual drunken stupors and was going to take it out on me. It was nothing new. I tried to fight back like I usually did, but I was a squirrely little teenager and I couldn't put up much of a fight. My mother butted in as she did from time to time and he took his anger out on her, also. She was always trying to shield me. A mother's instinct to protect her child is a strong one, if not always realistic. He grabbed her shirt with one hand and with the other he hit her in the face again and again. I can still remember every single blow like it was yesterday. A trickle of blood had run from her nose and smeared across her face as he hammered her.

"The tipping point was her eyes. They went dead. I had never seen a dead person before, but I knew right then that she was either dead or going to die if I didn't do something. I ran into the kitchen, grabbed the longest knife I could find and did what I had to do to save my mother.

"My father, knife blade protruding from his chest, turned and stared at me in amazement.

His mouth was opening and closing, but no words were coming out. Just a wheeze and a cough with a spray of bright red blood. That was the moment, that was the moment that changed my life. I don't know if you call it revelation or epiphany or what; but in his face I saw myself. I saw myself becoming that man, becoming that evil. In those last few moments, I think he saw himself in me. I think he looked at my face, red with the droplets of his life's blood, and knew that he had authored his own fate. We both looked into a mirror and that mirror gave us both a glimpse into Hell. It was too late for him. He died with a look of horror on his face that I never care to see on another human being.

"I didn't fight the authorities when they came; I knew I had done wrong. I went to prison and found religion! Well, everybody finds God in prison, but I really felt his presence in me. Over time I came to understand Him and to love Him. Eventually, I knew that he wanted me to spread His word. I felt the need, if for nothing more than my own redemption. I mean, God grants all of us forgiveness if we ask him for it. I've asked the Lord's forgiveness and have been hopefully granted with it, but I'm just a man with this burden on my heart. So, in order to seek God's favor, I lied to enter His service.

"After about six months with the mission at Santos, I was recalled. God forgives, but I guess the True Church does not. They somehow found out about my past and reclaimed my license to minister. I received a summons to return to Holy City to stand trial."

"But he never went!" Barabbas interjected once more. "He disappeared with a bunch of refugees and was never seen again. Not until now! Do you still have that…?"

A beeping sounded from the bishop's waistband. He pulled a communicator free and put it to his ear. The room was dead silent as Barabbas listened to his message. He closed his device, pocketed it and made an announcement to the room. "The Transit Authority is here and they want to speak to you. To all of you."

5

There was once a man who was in a flood. Rains poured down for weeks on end and a nearby river began to overflow its banks. The brown water crept closer and closer to his house until it began to leak inside. The man got down on his knees and prayed to the lord, but the water kept coming. When he could no longer kneel inside his home, he climbed onto his roof and continued praying. Before long a boat full of rescue workers came by. They offered to drive him to safety, but the man refused. He said, "No, I'm waiting on the lord to save me." The boat left and the man continued praying. Rain continued to fall from the sky and the water completely covered his house.

The rushing current threatened to sweep him away as he knelt upon his roof, but he continued to pray. Another boat, seeing him in trouble came to help. The men begged him to climb in so they could rescue him and again he refused. He said "I'm waiting on the lord to save me." The water continued to rise and before long, only his head was above the surface.

A helicopter, seeing the man in distress, came close and a rope ladder was lowered. A man in a helmet climbed down and lowered his arm. He said "Take my hand and I'll pull you up!"

"No," the man said a third time. "I'm waiting on the lord to save me." With that, the helicopter left. The water continued to rise and the man drowned.

When he died, he found himself in Heaven, bowing before God and a host of angels. He said, "My God, I prayed and I prayed and I asked for you to rescue me. I don't question your judgment, Lord, but I need to know, why did you not save me?"

God said, "I sent you two boats and a helicopter."

***

That story was swirling through my mind as I sat at the table with Bishop Barabbas and the rest of the crew of the Damascus.

Captain Stark was very unsettled. "The Transit Authority is here? What? Why did you let them in?"

Jenna stood up from the galley table and began to pace. She crossed her arms, uncrossed them and then crossed them again with her hands on her shoulders. Her fur began to take on a pale hue. "I don't like this. I don't like this one bit."

Barabbas leaned back and rubbed his top lip. His composure was iron. "Sanctuary is neutral, not exclusive. They can come and go as they want, but I assure you they have no jurisdiction here."

"So, what now? You're just going to let them arrest us?" The Captain was furious.

The Bishop leaned forward with his elbows on the table, meeting the captain eye to eye. "I'm not giving you to them, but I am obliged to facilitate a meeting if you're willing."

James was the next one to speak. "And what if they try to arrest us?"

"They can't." The Bishop almost seemed like he was beginning to get perturbed. "They're not even allowed weapons. Our own elite Temple Guard manages security." He turned back to the captain. "Jedediah, I highly suggest you meet with them so we can put this behind us."

"You meet with them."

"What?"

"You meet with them. You got us into this mess, so it's up to you to get us out."

Barabbas wrinkled his brow. "I didn't kill a transit authority worker."

Captain Stark raised one hand and put his finger in the bishop's face. "You bought the girls; you paid me to bring them to a safe place. You told me it would be alright. They boarded my ship because somebody told them I was running prostitutes. If it wasn't for your involvement, none of this would have ever happened. You got us into this mess, you get us out!"

That was a development I didn't expect. I couldn't keep my willful mouth shut. "You bought hookers?"

That took the bishop back a step or two. I definitely stepped on a raw nerve with that one. Obviously agitated, he turned to me and raised his voice. "Stay out of this Mozel, this doesn't concern you!"

Captain Stark realized the opportunity that had just presented itself. The bishop had suddenly been put in check by a rook and it was time to advance his knight. "Jacob is a trusted member of my crew and anything that concerns me concerns him, too. And this concerns me a great deal."

"There are no churches on Mo'ak." I didn't know if I was talking to myself or anyone else in the room, but the words came from my mouth all the same. Pieces were staring to come together in my mind, but I didn't have them all yet.

"I wasn't there. The church bought the girls to give them a better life. They asked to be taken away from all that and your captain was hired to take them to a safe place. Purchasing them was the only way to do it and not get shot by the brothel masters. I had hoped these would only be the first of many."

But, there are no churches on Mo'ak. Rook takes queen. It was time to put his king in check.

I knew I was speaking out of turn, but there was no other choice at the moment. "We'll meet with the Transit Authority, but only with you and an entire squad of Temple Guardsmen in the room."

Captain Stark turned on me. "Just who do you think you are?"

I looked him square in the eye. "Trust me."

We stayed like that for what seemed like an eternity.

Barabbas broke the silence. "Well, Captain? What's it going to be? The Transit

Authority is waiting inside as well as outside. You'll never get out of here except through this meeting."

Jedediah turned back towards him. "So, you would sell us out? We bring you the cargo you ask for and you would sell us out?"

"I'm not selling you out." The bishop regained his self-control, all except for a nervous little tick in his right index finger. I had seen it in him before when we played cards back in school. If I had any doubt before, it was gone now. "I'm simply seeking out a peaceful means to an end."

Captain Stark nodded his head. "Very well, Jenna and I will meet them in ten minutes."

The bishop shook his head. "No good, they say they have to meet with all of you."

Stark cast a glance at me and I nodded slightly. "Alright then, we'll arm up and meet them in twenty minutes. David, show this man to the aft hatch."

"No." The Bishop stood firm. "No arms in Sanctuary. Only the Temple Guard carry weapons here."

There was another tense moment of silence. Stark tensed his mouth and bowed his head in concession. With that, the Bishop was off of the Damascus.

***

When we finally exited the ship, a group of Temple Guards was waiting there to escort us to the meeting room. While the hallways and corridors were strictly functional in their purpose, the room where we were to talk was extravagant. The ceiling must have been twelve feet tall and huge pillars of carved oak lined the walls at regular intervals. Oak, so hard to come by since the trees were extinct and yet there was so much of it.

At either end of the meeting room was elegant gold carvings of Adam and Eve in the garden surrounded by all manner of animals and cherubs with harps flying through the air. In stark contrast to the bright room was the long mahogany table that had the Transit Authority and General Sanders sitting along one side. The guards took their place at either end of the room and the Bishop appeared, standing behind a large chair at the end of the table. He raised one arm, palm up, in our general direction. "Please, have a seat. I'll moderate and this will be over very soon."

We all sat down very slowly and the room was as quiet as a temple. Jenna's fur had returned to a deep scarlet hue. Her tail eased through the hole in the back of her seat and twitched twice before she settled in.

General Sanders patted the table with both hands and spoke first. "Okay, somebody has to start here. I'm placing you all under arrest for smuggling prostitutes."

Captain Stark leaned on to one elbow and pointed at him. "Now, wait a minute." He swung his finger around to the clergy as he spoke. "The Bishop paid us to move them as part of a relief effort. We were taking them to a safe place."

Barabbas wrinkled his brow, "What are you talking about?"

Captain Stark was dumbfounded. "I'm talking about you! You paid us to move the girls to Earth so you could help them. You told me yourself! Prostitution didn't even exist on Mo'ak until five years ago and you were trying to keep it from gaining a foothold!"

The Bishop sat up a little straighter at the accusations. He looked back and forth between Stark and the General. "This is all news to me. Captain, I don't know what type of game you're playing here, but you need to stop making excuses for your crimes."

The last piece of the puzzle fell into place in my head. I saw the scheme coming full circle now. I couldn't hold it in any longer. I stood up and raised my voice. "You took the girls and sold them into prostitution!"

The room was quiet at my outburst and all eyes were on me.

"There were no prostitutes on Mo'ak just like there were no churches! You had to make a crisis that you could solve in order to move in and take money from that planet just like you do all over the galaxy!"

The Bishop rose to his feet. "Mozel, I don't know where you're getting these hair brained stories, but I suggest you stop right now." His hands were shaking. If I needed confirmation that I was right, that was it.

"You created this mess and now these good people are going to prison so you can exploit a helpless planet! You need to stop right now!"

I looked down at Captain Stark; sweat was beading up on his forehead. He began to rise but was interrupted by General Sanders. "Sit down, Captain!"

Captain Stark didn't listen. I didn't think he would. Everything that happened next seemed to go in slow motion, although it was faster than anyone could imagine.

General Sanders leaned forward in his chair and put his right hand down onto his hip. The motion was suspicious, but the sound he made was unmistakable. He and the rest of the Transit Authority stood up into a crouched position, their side arms drawn and in the ready position.

Captain Stark looked at the Bishop. "I thought you said no guns!"

The Bishop's face was stern.

"I said sit down, Captain!"

Knowing that the situation was not going to end well, Jenna was the next of our crew on her feet. David and I were standing up when James, the hulk of a man he was, placed both hands under our side of the long mahogany table. With a growl that could only come from a bear or James Jessup, he began to push the heavy wood up and away from us. The last we saw of General Sanders was him and his men stumbling backwards as the heavy wood was leveraged against them.

Shots rang through the room as the Transit Authority officers discharged their pistols and bullets penetrated the high ceiling in the meeting room. Without thinking, I pushed on the table, too. I didn't know if my old body would even make a difference, but I had to do something. Looking to the side, I could see that the rest of the crew was following our lead and pushing the big heavy table back. Together, we pinned the officers against the far wall.

From the side of the table that was now up in the air, all we could see was one hand with a pistol in it, flailing blindly. It discharged once, twice and then a third time. Captain Stark yelled as he went for the gun and wrestled it away from the hidden person. "Run! Run! Get to the ship!" The Palace Guards were already pointing their rifles at us and taking aim. We didn't have to be told twice.

Jenna was the first one out the door with me following. James was behind us, but I didn't see him as much as I heard him. "Don't look back, just go!"

We ran down the alley towards the hangar where our own sanctuary was waiting for us. Three Temple Guards emerged from around a corner and placed their hands on their holsters at the sight of us. They didn't have time to draw.

With reflexes I'd never seen before, Jenna slapped the first one and followed through bringing her long arm down and behind the man's knee. She pulled up and he fell back, cracking his head on the hard floor. He was still alive, but he would have a terrible headache when he woke up. In a haze of arms, legs and bright red fur, she dispatched the other two before they could fire a shot.

I looked back to see James standing behind me, holding onto his brother, David, who was leaning over and clutching at his heart. Rivulets of blood were pouring out from around his fingers as he was trying desperately to hold his life in. More than a few bullets had caught him square in the chest. He slumped down out his brother's grasp. "I can't run anymore, get out of here!"

James was crying, mouth wide open making a sound I hope I never have to hear again. "No! I'm taking you with me!"

The only thing louder than the crying was a fresh round of gunshots as Captain Stark came running around the corner. He stopped to fire two more rounds down the hallway and ran in our direction once again. "We have to go now!"

That was enough for James, with tears in his eyes; he stumbled away from David and quickly paced up to a run.

We were almost to the hangar. I heard more shots and bullets ricocheted all around our heads. Flashes of sparks danced all around us. I raised my arms high in a defensive posture. I didn't think it would protect me from the bullets, but it somehow made me feel more secure.

The hatch to the Damascus was still open. I thanked God that we had a captain with good foresight. We shuffled in and I turned just in time to see Stark with his back to the wall outside of the corridor. He turned, fired two shots down the hallway and threw the gun down. He was out of ammo.

Jenna was in the driver's seat powering up the engines before the Captain was even in and closing the hatch. "Let's go! Let's go! Let's go!" He pushed past me and climbed the stairs to the upper level as I paused to catch my breath. My chest weighed a ton and the air seemed so thick I could barely breathe.

chunk chunk chunk chunk chunk

The familiar sound of gunfire on metal filled my ears and it was enough to motivate me up the stairs and into the cockpit. I lost my balance and fell over as the ship rose into the air and banked towards the exit. The Mo'ak girls were still in the galley. I could hear them crying. I yelled out as I found my seat and buckled down. "Girls! Find something to grab onto!"

The Damascus roared into life as Jenna punched the engines. The old ship started towards the hangar doors just as they began to close. The familiar sound of lead on steel still echoed from the rear hatch.

chunk chunk chunk chunk chunk

We were getting closer as the ship sped up, but the large bay doors were closing fast.

"We're not gonna make it! We're not gonna make it!" James yelled out in an uncharacteristic bout of panic.

"We're not going to make it!" Jenna screeched at the top of her cat lungs.

Stark, sitting in the captain's seat at her side. looked over at her and calmly said "I told you I would always take care of you. Today is no exception. Now, you're going to make it."

Still picking up speed, the nose of the ship peeked out into space with the doors still closing. All we could see on the front view now was black and stars. I thought we were home free. I thought wrong.

We were all jarred forward as the massive doors clamped shut on the ship.

Captain Stark was horrified. "Give it more! Give it more!"

Jenna's coat had turned back to a pale white. "I've got the throttle all the way!"

The ship's one remaining engine roared as they tried to push the Damascus free of its trap.

chunk chunk chunk chunk chunk

A deafening screech filled the cabin. It was steel tearing steel. If we got out of the mess we were in, I wondered if the ship would even be space worthy.

There are times when all that we do is not enough. I didn't know if we were right or we were wrong, but I knew that we had been lied to and that we had been manipulated and then we had been threatened with our lives. It was time for me to stop being afraid and place our safety in the hands of God.

chunk chunk chunk chunk chunk

The girls were screaming and the crew was yelling. Bullets continued to assault the ship from all sides now and the terrible metal on metal sound cried out again.

I cleared all of them from my mind, unbuckled my belt and got down on my knees. "Lord, I worship you and I praise you. If it is your will that I meet you today, I will rejoice in your decision. I will not question your actions. I feel you sent me to this ship for a reason. If I still have a duty to perform, please pull back those gates and release the ship."

There was a hand on my shoulder. It was one of the Mo'ak girls. Her eyes were wide and wet with tears. "Can I pray to your god, too?"

"Yes."

The bullets were still flying all around us and Stark was yelling at Jenna to push the engines harder. The little girl stared at me. "I don't know how."

chunk chunk chunk chunk chunk

I took her hand. "All you have to do is kneel down and ask God to be your lord and savior."

"But, I've done very bad things."

"That's okay. You will be washed in the blood of the lamb and born again and all of your sins will be wiped away."

She knelt down and began to pray. One by one, the other girls, who had been watching dropped to their knees and began to pray.

A ripping sound louder than any we had heard before filled the cockpit and we all fell backwards as the Damascus leaped out into open space.

The rear view screen was up and I could see Sanctuary getting smaller and smaller behind us. The landing bay doors were ripped and torn like paper.

We were silent for a long time. It might have been days, it seemed like it. Just sitting there taking in all that had just happened to us.

Jenna adjusted some dials and looked over at Captain Stark. "Where do we go now?"

He placed a hand on her far temple, pulled her close and kissed the top of her head.

"We go to Inillia. It would seem that we're smugglers again."